D0259576

This Little Tiger book belongs to:

_____

_____

_____

It's Mine!

Tracey Corderoy   Caroline Pedler

LITTLE TIGER PRESS
London

Lulu had come to play
with Baby Bear.

"I'm playing tigers with Rory," said Baby Bear.

"I *love* tigers!" cried Lulu. "Can I play?"

"Oooh, yes!" Baby Bear smiled.

"Look, I've made a den!"

"I can roar louder than you!" giggled Lulu.
"Raaghh!"
"Raaghh!" roared Baby Bear. And they
roared and roared and *roared*.

Suddenly Baby Bear's tummy rumbled. "We need tiger-snacks!" he said. So he hurried off to find some.

But when he came back ...

… Lulu was playing with Rory!

"Wheeee!" giggled Lulu, with a big tiger grin.

"Lulu! Stop!" cried Baby Bear. "Rory doesn't *like* swinging!"

Baby Bear grabbed
Rory's leg. Lulu held
on tight.

"But … Rory's … *mine!*"
puffed Baby Bear.

Baby Bear tugged.
Lulu tugged back *until* …

CRASH!

Then Lulu
started to cry.

"Baby Bear!" said Mummy, hurrying in.
"You need to *share* your toys."

Slowly, Baby Bear held out
another toy for Lulu.

"But I don't want *him*," Lulu
frowned. "I want *Rory*."

"Why don't we go to the park?"
smiled Mummy. "I'll bring Rory
along with *me*."

"OK," mumbled Baby Bear
and Lulu.

When they got there, Lulu stomped to the
see-saw and Baby Bear plodded to the swings.

But Lulu's see-saw wasn't
much fun. It wouldn't go up and down.
Baby Bear's swing wasn't much fun either.
It wouldn't go forwards and backwards!
　　After a while, Lulu wandered over
to Baby Bear…

"I can push you if you like?" she said.
"Yes, please!" smiled Baby Bear.
Lulu pushed the swing, a little
at first. Then higher and higher
and **higher!**

"Wheeee!"
chuckled Baby Bear.
And *then* he had an idea.

Baby Bear scrambled off
the swing and dashed
across to Mummy.

"Lulu! Lulu!" he cried,
racing back…

"*You* have Rory," said Baby Bear. "He says
he *loves* swinging now!"
"Let's push him together!" Lulu smiled.

"Or I could push all *three* of you," said Mummy,
"so you can *share* the swing."

"Higher! Higher!"
they giggled.

"Time to go!" said Mummy at last. "I've got
a big treat for you at home…"

"*Ice-cream!*" cheered
Baby Bear and Lulu. Then they
both sang...

"Friends together — one, two, three...
Sharing ice-cream for our tea!
Drippy, soft and yummy too,
Some for me and some for you!"

For my lovely niece, Jemima ~ T C xx

For twins, Hallie and Dylan, and a lifetime of sharing ~ C P

LITTLE TIGER PRESS
1 The Coda Centre
189 Munster Road, London SW6 6AW
www.littletigerpress.com

First published in Great Britain 2012
This edition published 2013
Text copyright © Tracey Corderoy 2012
Illustrations copyright © Caroline Pedler 2012
Tracey Corderoy and Caroline Pedler have asserted their rights
to be identified as the author and illustrator of this work
under the Copyright, Designs and Patents Act, 1988
A CIP catalogue record for this book
is available from the British Library

ISBN 978-1-84895-482-3
Printed in China
LTP/1800/0566/0313
2 4 6 8 10 9 7 5 3 1

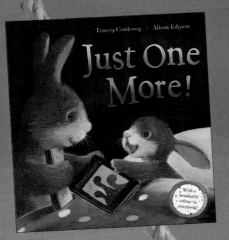